MEAT LOAD

CAPRICORN COVE SERIES

EVIE MITCHELL

This book is a work of fiction. Names, characters, places, incidents, facts, and sometimes random sentences are either the product of the author's imagination or are used in what she hopes is an entirely flattering but fictitious manner. Any resemblance to actual persons, living or dead, or actual events, and locales is entirely coincidental.

Editor: Nicole Wilson, Evermore Editing
http://www.evermoreediting.wixsite.com/info
Cove Illustration by Laras Putri

ACKNOWLEDGEMENT OF COUNTRY

I acknowledge the Traditional Custodians of the lands on which I write, the Ngunnawal people, and pay my respect to elders both past and present.

I acknowledge the continued and deep spiritual relationship of the Australian Aboriginal and Torres Strait Islander peoples' to this land, and their unique cultural and spiritual relationships to the land, waters and seas and their rich contribution to society.

Always was, always will be.

*To spelling errors, Janeane, and my greedy readers
Without whom, Meat Load would not have been
born.*

*And as always—to my husband.
I'm always ready for your meat load.*

MEAT LOAD

Hannah
He's hilarious.
He's fun.
He's not into me.

Malik
She's serious.
She's proper.
I'm into her.

This is one loaded relationship.

Warning: This book is inspired by gorgeous women, hilarious men, and the kind of love that makes you swoon.

PROLOGUE

Malik

Halloween

Hannah Sharp had always intrigued me. Back in school, they'd labelled her the mean girl. The frigid ice bitch who could snap off a man's penis with a withering glance. She'd ruled our school, laying to waste those who crossed her with an efficient, cutting remark.

To be honest, I'd never seen her as any of that and had repeatedly vocalised my disappointment with people who spoke about her in those terms.

Hannah definitely had an ice-queen look about her, sure. The white-blonde hair, the stunning blue eyes, her pale skin. She tended to wear muted colours—white, black, navy—which no doubt emphasised the effect. But where other people saw cold and standoffish, I saw awkward and unsure. And, maybe, a little scared. As if she weren't sure what she was doing or how to do it.

I'd worked with enough kids over the years to spot an abuse case, and Hannah fit the profile. Reserved, untrusting, desperate for affection.

I wanted to wrap her up in a sushi blanket roll and cuddle her for days.

Case in point—Hannah had never participated in a scavenger hunt. She'd never played 'never have I ever', or 'truth and dare'. Had never even attended a school party.

Which made tonight extra special.

"We did well, didn't we?" she asked, once again admiring our junk piece of a trophy as it glinted in the firelight.

"Hundred percent. We make a great team."

Our annual Halloween scavenger hunt had seen my friendship group pair off, each of us competing for the ultimate prize—a shitty trophy that was little more than pieces of junk glued together and spray-painted gold.

I coveted that trophy like a man covets treasure—with a nearly overwhelming need for it to be mine.

The annual scavenger hunt had been a staple in my life since my early years when my mother—at her wit's end—had decided that the best way for kids to work off their Halloween sugar high was through a scavenger hunt. The competition had been run every year since. This year was only the fifth time I'd managed to win.

And it's all thanks to Hannah.

"You should keep it this year," I said, tipping my beer bottle toward the trophy. "Rule is you have to display it somewhere prominent in your house. And next year, when you bring it back, it has to be updated with some new addition that reminds us of this hunt."

She flushed, her head dipping down as she looked away. "I'm not sure if I'll be invited next year."

"What?" I scoffed, shaking my head. "Reigning champions must defend their title, and you, Hannah Sharp, are a master at scavenger hunts. A veritable savant."

She grinned, her blush deepening. "Thank you, Malik."

I waved a hand dismissively as Farrah rejoined our fire-pit circle.

"Hey, Sharif, how's it feel to be runner-up?" I asked, unable to resist teasing my roommate.

I knew my twin sister was hoping Farrah and I would hook up, but considering they'd been best friends since their tween years, it would be like kissing a relative. Farrah and I were just fine as friends and roommates.

The woman in question flicked me the bird, poking her tongue out and muttering an expletive that involved a creative use for my genitals.

I chuckled, incredibly pleased to have finally broken Farrah's winning streak.

"To Hannah and Malik!" Yasmin, my twin, raised her beer in a toast.

Around the fire pit sat some of my closest friends. In addition to Hannah, Farrah, and Yasmin, there was Caleb Prince—my best friend in the goddamn world, and Wolf Rodriguez—who was currently dressed as Spiderman, complete with mask, in an effort to avoid detection.

Must be hard being a world-famous rock star. Can't even share a beer with friends without being mobbed.

I shuddered.

I cannot think of any job I'd like less than that. Give me anonymity any day.

As the night wore on, the childish games became more outrageous.

"Alright, what should we play next?" Yasmin

asked, laughing at Farrah's mutinous expression. "How about truth or dare?"

Hannah pressed her lips together, her face taking on a slightly pinched look.

Uh-oh.

"How does it work?"

We all turned toward her.

"I'm sorry?"

"Truth or dare. How does it work? I haven't played before."

"No way in hell you've never played this game!" Yasmin declared, pointing a finger emphatically at Hannah. "Seriously, this is like *the game* we played in high school."

I felt Hannah stiffen beside me, her breath catching.

I opened my mouth, about to try and smooth over the situation, when Hannah shrugged.

"I didn't really attend high school parties."

"Well, consider this a trip down memory lane," I told her, slapping a hand on my knee. "And I"—I pressed my palm to my chest—"shall graciously go first."

I looked at my best friend, giving him an evil eyebrow lift.

"Truth or dare, Caleb?"

He lifted his beer bottle, shooting me a grin. "Truth."

He took a swig while I pursed my lips, taking an exaggerated pause, attempting to put Hannah at ease.

See? It's just a game.

"Is it true that you got to shake Wayne Gretzky's hand, or was that bullshit?"

He chuckled as Farrah and Yasmin groaned, rolling their eyes.

"It's true, you motherfucker, and you know it. Your turn."

"Shoot," I said, stretching my arms out in welcome. "Hit me with your best shot."

"I dare you to eat the last stuffed jalapeño."

I leaned over to Hannah. "Now, I can either accept the dare—or if he'd been a decent person—the truth he's asking for, or I can refuse."

"What happens if you refuse?"

"Normally, we have to do a task we don't want to."

"Like stay and clean up after the party," Caleb butted in. "So, what's it gonna be, Officer El Khoury?"

"I'll do it."

I shoved off my seat, strolling to the table to pluck the hot jalapeño from its lonely place on the plate.

"Be kind to me tomorrow," I ordered, shoving it

in my mouth. Heat burst across my tongue, tears blurring my vision as I questioned whether Satan was a mythical beast or the food in my mouth.

"Malik's a wuss when it comes to heat," my traitor of a sister explained to Hannah. "Can't stand anything hotter than the mildest of peppers."

I reached for a glass of water, sucking it down as the jalapeño slid down to burn an ulcer in my belly.

I've made a huge mistake.

The watching crowd of my former friends laughed as I suffered through the initial burn, gasping and gulping water.

Do I ask for milk? No, surely not. You can do this, El Khoury. You got this. Suck it up. SUCK IT UP!

Breathing through my mouth, I returned to the fire, attempting to dab discretely at the sweat on my brow.

Hannah leaned in, offering me a fresh glass of water. "You okay?"

I nodded, still unable to speak without breathing fire.

"My turn!" Farrah leaned forward. "Truth or dare, Yazzy?"

"Truth."

Hannah watched wide-eyed as around and

around the circle they went, truths and dares coming hard and fast.

"Okay, your turn," Yasmin told Hannah with a grin. "Truth or dare, Hannah?"

Hannah wore a pumpkin pinned to her head and a shirt that had the number 3.1415926535897932384626433... and so on written across it.

Pumpkin pie. Classic.

She pursed her lips, her stunning blue eyes giving nothing away. "Dare."

"Ooohhh! She's got lady balls!" I yelled, pretending to act shocked.

You go girl!

"Alright, I dare you...."

My stomach grumbled, reminding me that I hadn't eaten anything since the jalapeño. Three of Hannah's home-baked chocolate fudge cookies sat on a plate near the fire.

Just one won't hurt.

I paused, considering the offerings.

Actually, I've been good, I deserve this treat. And it really wouldn't be fair to leave a man, or in this case, a cookie behind.

I reached for them as Yasmin finished her dare.

"I dare you to take those cookies from Malik and give them to me."

My head jerked up, my hand frozen halfway to my mouth, the cookies so close and yet so far.

"Excuse me?" I asked, bristling with indignation. "What the fuck, Yaz?"

She giggled, nodding at Hannah. "Go on, Hannah! Quick! Before he eats them."

Hannah nodded, holding out a hand to me. "I'll take those, please, and thank you."

Excuse me?

"What? No!"

Hannah frowned. "It's my dare. Are you not going to help me with my dare?"

"Nope." I moved to stuff the cookies in my mouth, but Hannah was faster. Her hand shot out, gripping and twisting my wrist, snatching the falling cookies from the air.

"What the fuck!?" I howled, cradling my wrist as pain flared. "Where'd you learn that?"

"Dojo," Hannah replied, cradling the cookies in a napkin. She stood, walking toward a cackling Yasmin, who had tears running down her cheeks. "Here you go... Yazzy."

Over my dead body.

I surged to a stand, scooping Hannah up, preventing her from handing the cookies off to my traitor sister. With a practised heave, I tossed her over my shoulder and headed off into the dark shadows at the back of Caleb's yard.

"Don't come looking for us!" I yelled over my shoulder. "We're negotiating cookies!"

The group's laughter trailed after us as I carried us away.

Away from the fire, the darkness embraced us, the only light coming from the moon above. At the very back of the yard, I helped Hannah slide off my shoulder, the napkin-wrapped cookies still clasped in her hands.

"Alright, Ms. Sharp, hand them over." My grin faded as I took her in.

She stood frozen, her face pale, her eyes glassy.

"Hannah?" I reached out to touch her, but she sprang backward, stumbling to get away.

Oh, fuck.

"Hannah?"

She raised both hands, one still holding the cookies. "Please don't touch me."

I blinked, swallowing. "Sorry. I didn't think. Shit, sorry, Hannah. I should have realised how inappropriate it was to just heave you around. I do it all the time to Yazzy and Farrah. I just didn't think. Sorry."

She sucked in a breath, turning slightly away from me, her hair covering her expression.

"Thank you for your apology."

I nodded, feeling like a complete dick. "Are you okay?"

She remained silent, breath misting in the cool night air.

"I will be." She turned, her blue eyes searching my face. "I don't like being touched."

The way she said it sounded off.

You fucking jackass. Way to impress the woman you like.

"Is there anything I can do?"

She shook her head. "I'm feeling over-whelmed. Please give me a moment."

I nodded, hovering awkwardly.

Shit. Shit. Shit. Shit. You done gone and fucked up, Malik.

"Shall we go back to the fire?" Hannah asked after a moment.

"Um, sure. If that's what you want."

"I do. I'm enjoying the games." She twisted on her heel, heading to the fire.

I fell in beside her, glancing over.

"I really am sorry, Hannah."

She nodded. "I know."

And with that, we returned to the fire, games, and pretending nothing had happened between us.

1

Hannah

"Hey, all you Pretty Pollys out there, welcome to the first episode of the Wicked Women podcast for the new year. I'm Karen Q, and I'm here with my co-host—"

I leaned into the microphone, smiling as I announced myself. "Mistress H."

"—to discuss all things feminist, feminine, and fine as fuck!"

Five years ago, I'd met Karen at a bookstore. We'd both been searching for the romance section only to be told the store had recently removed all romance books from sale. Their reason being that romance didn't sell. I'd been halfway through telling the owner the facts about romance being the workhorse of the book world and a multi-billion-dollar industry when Karen had interrupted.

"And it's feminist as fuck!" she'd declared, stamping her foot. "Women writing about women pleasure. Consent. Love. Not to mention becoming more LGBTIQA+ inclusive, disability-inclusive, and CALD-inclusive. I mean, who doesn't want a romance?"

We'd left the store after the owner had threatened to call the police. We'd met for coffee, discussed books, and then headed off to lunch. A few months later, over our weekly coffee date, the Wicked Women podcast had been born. Now we were four seasons in and had a listenership of over 10 million.

Karen flashed me a smile as our intro music wrapped up. "Mistress H, tell me, how were your holidays? Did you conquer the dreaded Christmas family dinner?"

I sighed, shaking my head as remembered anxiety twisted in my gut. "No. Despite all efforts to be civil, dinner disintegrated into a melee of words between my father, his new girlfriend, and my aunt."

I'd flown down to the South Island to visit my dad. He'd moved down there when he'd retired as Capricorn Cove's sheriff, deciding he needed a fresh start somewhere far away from my mother. The joke was on him—my mother had moved to LA a month later.

Thanksgiving had been messy. My aunt and father had never gotten along. I still wasn't sure why he'd invited her, but it had quickly escalated, and I'd been stuck in the middle. Again.

Karen winced. "Ouch. Was it entertaining, at least?"

"For the first two hours, then the cops arrived. After that, it was just me bailing my aunt out of jail and dealing with paperwork for the next six hours."

And what a fun day that was. Such a waste of time and effort.

Karen hit the sad sound button, causing me to grin. "That sounds like the worst Christmas you've had since the one where someone ate your dessert."

"It was. At least this time, I got pudding."

We chatted about our holidays before cutting to a commercial break, Chrissy, our producer, now dialling into the web call.

"And we're back," Karen said into the microphone. "It's time to introduce our guest for this week. She's our producer, a mum-to-be, a kickass boss lady, and one of the best friends I've ever had. Let's give it up for Christine!"

Karen unmuted Christine's call as I waved.

"Chrissy-boo, how are you?" she asked, blowing her air kisses.

"Fat, fun, and fine as fuck." Christine laughed, holding her hand up to the screen for a virtual high-five.

"May I remind you that you're pregnant?" I asked, flicking a chunk of hair out of my face. "Fat is not a descriptor I'd use for the beauty of your body right now."

I wish it was me.

"Mistress, I love you, but you are dead wrong." Christine leaned back, patting her eight-month-pregnant belly. "I am *so* done with being pregnant. It feels as if my ankles are about to explode. If I don't get some foot massages up in here, I'm worried I may never walk again."

"I'd just like to remind you of something you said at the start of this single mum journey. What was it? Oh, that's right." Karen made her voice wispy and overly high-pitched. "Pregnancy is a gift, and I can't wait to experience it all. And best of all, I don't have to share it with anyone else!"

Chrissy groaned. "I hate that you remember that."

"Babe, I remember everything."

We all cackled, then I glanced at the time,

quickly lifting my run schedule, determined to keep us on track.

"Chrissy, your email was incredibly cryptic. All it says is that you want to talk to us about resolutions."

"Uh-huh." She leaned forward, grinning into the computer screen. "I've decided it's time to shake up this little podcast. You ladies have had enough of being safe at home hiding behind your microphones. I've decided it's time to get you out from behind the desk and into the big bad world."

Karen blinked. "Huh?"

"What are you asking us to do?" I asked, raising an eyebrow.

Christine rubbed her hands together. "I've signed you both up for a few new year's resolutions."

"What?"

"Why?" I asked.

"You can't do that!"

"This is a horrible idea!"

"I hate people!" Karen wailed.

"You know Karen hates people."

She made a quiet motion with her hands. "Look, I get it. It's a big scary world filled with people you might hate. But ladies, you're Wicked Women. And Wicked Women don't settle. They don't stay at home when there are challenges to be slain. They get out there and take names. And that's what I want you to do."

She clicked her screen, sharing it with us. "I asked the listeners over the holidays to send us their bucket lists. From that, I've pulled the things that are in the local area. Over the next few months, we're going to tick them off one by one."

"I'm sorry, does that say zip-lining?" Karen asked in horror.

"What exactly is a Brazilian cleanse?" I frowned at the screen, reading through the list.

Massages. Pole dancing. Meat load therapy... what the dickens is meat load therapy?

"Patience ladies, let me explain." Christine leaned into her microphone, dropping her voice an octave. "You'll thank me later."

I strongly disagree.

"I've signed you both up for things that I think you need. Mistress, you need more self-care, more vulnerability, more emotion, and more lightness in your life."

I cocked an eyebrow.

"Do I?"

"Yes." Christine gave a firm nod. "You do. That's why we've signed you up for different types of relaxation and emotional connection classes."

I glanced at the list. "But... meat load therapy? What is that? Is that an actual activity or a cooking class?"

"Oh, it looks amazing!" Christine enthused. "It's a new spa therapy that involves wrapping yourself in fur while a piece of steak is placed over your face. You then listen to the sounds of the forest while meditating. Apparently, it's very primal."

There was a beat of silence, Karen and I exchanging a glance via the computer screen.

"Let me get this straight. Mistress H is becoming a shish kebab while I try my luck at being a daredevil?" Karen asked. "Chrissy, this reads like a list of dumb ways to die. I mean, skydiving? Fuck. No."

She grinned. "I thought you'd say that, that's why I've already pre-purchased everything. All you need to do is turn up."

Stunned silence met her declaration.

Did she really just say....?

Karen must have read my mind. "I'm sorry. Can you repeat that?"

"All you need to do is turn up. All the details are in your emails right now."

"Mistress H, any thoughts?" Karen asked.

I closed my eyes, sucking in a deep breath. My therapist's soothing voice played through my head.

It's okay, Hannah. You've made great progress.

Don't worry about sounding weird. Just say what you want to say.

I let my breath out slowly. "I don't like surprises."

"Psh." Chrissy waved a dismissive hand. "Surprises are awesome."

"And," I continued. "I don't like being touched. This sounds like something *you* want, Christine. Not Karen or I."

Again, Christine dismissed me. "You'll enjoy it if you give it a chance."

Okay, this is becoming unacceptable.

"Christine," I began, attempting to sound impassive rather than emotional. "As you would be aware, consent is not something limited to sexual activity. It crosses all lines. In this instance, while you've offered something that sounds wonderful, you didn't seek consent to undertake this kind of decision. It's one thing to surprise someone. It's quite another to not accept that they don't wish to do it."

There was a moment of silence from Chrissy.

"Hard burn from Mistress H. Let's see how Chrissy retaliates," Karen whispered into the microphone.

We both ignored her.

Christine slowly shook her head. "So, you're saying I've overstepped?"

"Yes."

Duh.

Chrissy's eyes narrowed on me, her displeasure dripping down the screen. "Ex-cuse me?"

Patience, Hannah. You can do this.

"You made a decision—"

"You told me you were up for an adventure!"

My control snapped.

"I thought you meant one activity! One! And something that wouldn't involve touching!"

"You never said touching was an issue for you!"

"Touching is always an issue for me! How many times have we talked about it on this podcast?"

"Then it's good to challenge yourself."

"Boundaries!" I barked. "Boundaries, Chrissy! Some things you can't control. You need to respect where mine begin."

"I do respect you. I also recognise when a friend needs a push."

"This is—"

"Guys," Karen interrupted. "Ladies!"

We fell silent.

"What if we just give it a go?" she asked. "I mean, I could try zip-lining. And I could take one of the massages. Maybe between the both of us, we could just work out what we want to do."

I exhaled.

Just do it, Hannah. They don't ask a lot of you. And you can swap the touching stuff out with Karen.

"That will be fine," I said, my tone implying it was anything but.

"Except for the meat load therapy," Chrissy said, waggling a finger at the screen. "That one is non-transferable."

Oh, for goodness sake!

"Fine," I snapped. "I shall be decked out in meat while listening to jungle sounds. Are you satisfied?"

Chrissy laughed, her eyes dancing with delight. "Yep."

"And Chrissy," Karen asked, a warning in her tone. "Next time you have a great idea like this, what will you do?"

She rolled her eyes. "I'll ask first. Even if I think it's for your own good."

"Thank you."

The prerecorded ads ended, and Karen leaned into her microphone, getting on with the show.

"Alright, so it's settled. We're off to zip-lining and meat therapy. Listeners, wish us luck 'cause Mistress H and I are pretty sure we're about to die."

Truer words have never been spoken.

2

Hannah

This can't be it.

I pulled my phone out, double-checking the directions I'd memorised last night.

Well, shit.

Back in the early seventies, a couple of free-loving individuals had decided to move out to Capricorn Cove and set up a commune. They'd settled by Lover's Lake, which sat up in the mountains, buying up tracts of land, and building bunkhouses, yoga studios, and the like.

Unlike some places, this wasn't a cult. It was run by two people who just wanted to offer a place for people to stay, connect to nature, and be at peace without judgment.

As the decades came and went, Lover's Lake Camp changed ownership a few times, first becoming a summer camp, then a proper campground.

Now it seemed the new owner had decided to take Lover's Lake Camp in a new direction. One I wasn't entirely sure I approved of.

"Hannah?"

I startled, jumping and twisting, my heart pounding through my chest.

Oh, dear.

Behind me, looking far too tempting, stood Malik.

"Hey," he said with an easy grin. "I thought that was you."

"What are you doing here?" I blurted the question out before I could even think to exchange pleasantries.

Malik rubbed his hands together, his expression eager, seeming not at all perturbed by my lack of finesse. "I'm here for the meat load therapy. Can't wait!"

My eyebrows shot up—no doubt high enough to disappear into my hairline. "You *want* to do this?"

"Of course. Who wouldn't?"

Me? Any sane person that doesn't wish to catch a blood-borne disease?

I opened my mouth to respond but was interrupted by the arrival of a woman of diminutive stature and giant dreadlocks. She wore a long, free-flowing dress, a multitude of crystal-beaded jewellery, and bare feet.

"Welcome to Lover's Lake Resort! I'm Maude, and you must be Hannah and Malik, my students for today. Welcome."

Malik held his hand out. "Hi Maude, I'm—"

"Oh, no." Maude shook her head, cutting him off. "I'm sorry. I'm undergoing an aural cleanse, and until we've already performed a smudging, I'm afraid I won't be able to touch you until you are also cleansed. Don't want to invite any hanger-on spirits, you know?"

Malik nodded as if this completely made sense. "Of course."

Of course? I'm so confused.

"Great. Let's start your treatment."

She twirled on one foot, her hair and dress flaring around her as she pranced toward a well-worn path that disappeared into the woods around us.

"After you," Malik said with a lavish bow.

I followed Maude, listening with one ear as she pointed out the various plant and animal life around us, hyper-aware of Malik at my back.

He leaned in, his voice soft as we paused, Maude crashing into the undergrowth to retrieve a handful of wild sage.

"This isn't how I was expecting today to start," he said with a soft chuckle. "With a hippy and the prettiest lady around."

Warmth unfurled at his words. "Thank you for the compliment."

He shrugged, his gaze lifting as we got to the end of the path.

"What in the...?"

I looked ahead, frowning as we entered a clearing, two huts sat on either side of the cleared space—their walls made of a mix of mud and grasses and the roof with branches thick with leaves.

My gaze strayed to the fire in the middle of the clearing where a man—a *naked* man— waved sage around the space, singing and jumping about.

I'm going to kill Chrissy.

"Um." Malik stumbled to a stop beside me. "I thought this was a class to learn how to do fire-based barbecue."

"Oh, no." Maude waved her hand. "That's the meat *life* course. They have classes here on Fridays. You know, this happens surprisingly often.

Anyway, our program is much better. We're here to cleanse our bodies and embrace our inner wild children!"

Malik and I exchanged bemused glances.

"And that involves a naked man?" I asked, eyeing the guy still flailing around the fire pit.

"Of course. We'll all be naked."

And with that declaration, she reached for the ties at the back of her neck, giving them a rough tug until the material fell down to pool at her hips, revealing her naked top half.

"Sorry, what's happening?" Malik squeaked beside me, his voice breaking as he began to back up a little.

"We're returning to nature just as we were born to it—naked, glorious, and wonderfully whole."

Maude stripped off the rest of her dress, tossing it to the side with a flourish, the material catching in the wind as it began a gentle glide to the ground.

I'm so going to kill Chrissy.

"I'm not sure I'm comfortable with—"

The man spotted us, streaking across the clearing to skid to a halt in front of us, the bundles of smouldering sage sending billows of white smoke tumbling toward us.

"Welcome! I'm Brian. I'll be your guide for today."

He began to circle us, waving the sage so the smoke would spill over our skin.

"Let's do an aural spirit cleansing to begin. You can disrobe as we start."

I exchanged a glance with Malik, who seemed to be a little flushed.

It's just a body, Hannah.

With a sigh, I reached for my shirt, gripping the hem and pulling it off in one movement.

Malik's flush deepened, his body shifting as he looked away.

"We're going to start with a smudging— though many of our Indigenous peoples have their own terms and phrases for this kind of ceremony," Brian explained as he walked around us, wafting the smoke. "It's used throughout the world in different contexts."

He stopped, bowing his head for a moment. "I'd like to first start by acknowledging the traditional owners of the land on which we meet and pay my respects to my elders, past and present. Please join me in paying your respects today."

Both Malik and I bowed our heads, and something warm settled in my gut as Brian began a patterned dance around us.

I'd been inclined to dismiss this as nothing more than a meaningless frivolity performed by two harmless but eccentric hippies. But as I disrobed, Maude and Brian began to explain their background and how they'd come to start the meat-load therapy.

They took the time to describe where each of the traditions came from—including how they differed across cultures, what their connection was to the practice, and how they'd come to be trained in it.

I found myself naked and fascinated by the ceremony, awed by their respect and their stories, their love of their culture, and their love of these practices.

"What was the dance you were doing earlier?" Malik asked, his hands cupped lightly in front of his cock as Maude and Brian continued to walk around us, the smoke gently coating our skin.

"Oh, that was just some twerking to Lizzo," Brian laughed. "Gotta keep these hips nimble."

I giggled as Maude moved in closer, beginning to fan the smoke directly onto my skin.

"You might like to say a prayer or hold a positive thought," she directed. "Some of our people like to call down the gods and ask for their protection. We're here to invite positive energy in and ask the negative energy to leave."

I hesitated, unsure of what to think. Then Malik turned, his big body graceful for such a bulky man. He caught my eye, grinning as he raised one hand to slap his stomach, his other hand attempting to preserve his modesty.

"Fat-strong," he said with a laugh. "Caleb gives me shit about it, but this body is perfect just as it is. Including the tendency to eat a cookie or two more than I need."

My lips raised in an answering smile, and a warm liquid feeling settled in my own belly, pleased to be invited into his joke.

Thick from his head to his toes, Malik was what I'd call a hot, husky hulk of a man. Hefty and deliciously broad, he looked gorgeous, his humour his most attractive characteristic.

Halloween night came back to me at that moment. The feel of his arm as he lifted me. The ease with which he carried me across the backyard. The sharp crack of desire I'd felt when he'd touched me.

It had been too much—far too much. My emotions had threatened to overwhelm me that night, teetering on the edge of chaos.

"Yes," Maude whispered as she crouched by my legs, wafting smoke around my knees. "Your aura just changed. Keep thinking that thought."

Malik.

He'd closed his eyes, a small smile on his face as Brian wafted smoke over his crown, down his neck, and across his broad shoulders. I stared, following the smoke trails as they glided across Malik's skin, down his chest, and across his thick belly.

I want to kiss his belly.

The thought was so startling, so incredibly unexpected, that I nearly jumped.

Years ago, I'd assumed recognised that I was different from my peers. I'd been described as frigid, cold, an ice queen. The names both devastating and traumatising—reinforcing my differentness.

When my father had finally retired as Capricorn Cove's local sheriff and moved south, I'd found myself at a loss. For years I'd looked after him, cooking and cleaning, ensuring he had what he needed before he needed it.

I'd once been told that acts of service might be my love language, but for a long time I'd felt that I was incapable of experiencing that elusive emotion.

I wasn't a demonstrative person. I didn't actively reach for hugs or compliment people. More often than not, what came out of my mouth seemed to be criticisms or words that were taken as such. It seemed I was always out of step with the world. Always a beat off from everyone else. The niceties that most people seemed to master I failed. I was always too straight, too strict, too rigid.

After a particularly nasty run-in with Blue

McKenney a few years ago stemming from a misunderstanding, I'd sought out a psychiatrist. I'd been attempting to offer advice to Blue, but the mental health professional had gently pointed out that Blue hadn't wanted or needed my help and that the words I'd used had been inherently harmful.

It was through my work with her that I'd come to realise I wasn't a broken being but rather disinterested in sex with others. I had an active self-sex drive, but when I looked at other people, I rarely felt that attraction zing.

Not until Malik.

After my father had moved and Sheriff Rodriguez had taken over the precinct, I'd started bringing them the cookies I'd used to bake for my dad. It might not have seemed like much, but I enjoyed cooking. The police had seemed appreciative, so I'd continued, then expanded to the firefighters and ambulance down the road. Now I had a full contingent of services I baked for.

It gave me joy, and—if I were honest with myself—it gave me an excuse to see Malik.

"That completes the smudging," Brian said softly, pulling me out of my fixation. "We'll go ready the huts, and when you feel comfortable, come join us."

They separated, one into each hut, leaving us standing, naked, in the clearing.

Malik shot me a grin. "Not how I thought today was going to go, but you know what? I'm having a great time."

My gaze dropped to his stomach once again. "Can I kiss your belly?"

3

Malik

The words hung awkwardly in the space between us.

She wants to...?

I sucked in a breath. "Hannah... what?"

Her big blue eyes stared at me for a moment, then blinked slowly.

"I want to kiss your stomach. You're the first real man I've been attracted to in quite some time. Can I?"

This woman who I'd fantasised about for months was offering to kiss my stomach? Was this a dream?

I glanced toward the huts, my cock beginning to harden under my cupped hands.

Shit, man. Pull it together.

"Here? Now?"

She nodded.

The image hit me hard—Hannah crouching before me, the sun shining off her perfectly styled blonde hair, her hands reaching out to brace on my thighs as she leaned forward, those gorgeous lips pursed as she leaned in, her breasts at the perfect height to—

"No!" The word burst forth before I could temper my tone.

"No?" Her face fell, her beautiful lips turning down. "What about other places? Can I touch —" She pointed to my groin.

My cock pulsed, my body celebrating.

Yes! Please!

"No—that is—no! I-I—no!" I stuttered and stumbled, naked, aroused, and far too full of burning heat to deal with even the thought of her placing a finger on me.

This is a public space! You could get arrested for public indecency. You should arrest yourself for public indecency! You can't just bend her over and—

"I-I-I gotta go!" I twisted on one heel, speeding toward the hut Brian had disappeared into.

Ice, snow, lettuce leaves, carrot sticks, hummus.

By the time I made it to the hut, I had a quickly dwindling erection and enough recriminations for how I'd just handled the woman of my dreams to serve me into the next decade.

You're a goddamned idiot. Turn around and go get her!

"Welcome brother," Brian greeted. He raised a giant fur pelt holding it out toward me. "Let's cloak you up."

Incense burned around us as Brian wrapped me in the stitched-together animal furs.

"Deer, rabbit, squirrel, even some feathers from our aerial friends," he said, pulling the furs tight around me. "All sourced ethically and sustainably. This is the first step to reconnect you to nature and your inner animal."

Pretty sure Hannah already did that for me.

Brian guided me around the hut three times, walking me through three different types of incense, each chosen to represent a different smell from nature.

"Now, we're going to lay you down and I'm going to place the fresh kill on your chest."

I lay down on a small bed of leaves, watching as he removed a steak from an ice chest.

"Close your eyes, listen to the sound of nature. Feel the meat, feel the skins around you, feel the furs and leaves. Reconnect to nature. I'll be back in half an hour to check in on you."

He placed the meat on my chest, then rose, quietly crossing to the door of the hut.

"And Malik?"

"Yeah?"

"Maybe next time, don't turn a woman like Hannah down."

Face burning, I closed my eyes and tried to concentrate on the meat and the smells and the... whatever the fuck this therapy was meant to be—anything but Hannah Sharp and how badly I'd fucked up.

Again.

4

Hannah

"Your turn Mistress H, how did the meat load therapy go?"

Karen and Chrissy smiled at me over the computer screens, their faces expectant.

It was a week on from the meat therapy and despite my best efforts, I still felt nothing but abject humiliation when I thought of the day.

I want to kiss your belly.

"Horrid." I groaned. "Christine, I blame you."

"For?" she asked, raising an eyebrow.

I dropped my head in my hands. "Everything."

Karen made a sympathetic sound. "Mistress, do we need to make this a safe sharing corner?"

I nodded, my head still in my hands.

"Alright, Wicked Women. Mistress H is asking for a safe space which means we're all here to support her. Shoot, Mistress."

We were recording our latest podcast episode, the one where we were meant to review the activities we did. Karen had scored a date with a hot-as-heck lumberjack while I was certain all I'd managed to do was fuck up one of only a few friendships in my life.

And freak out a perfectly nice man.

I groaned again, sucked in a breath then raised my head. "I might be attracted to someone. And he might not be attracted to me. In fact, I am certain he isn't."

Christine's eyes bugged out of her head. "How are you certain?"

"He said so."

Oh, boy did he say so.

Karen's eyebrows shot up. "I'm sorry?"

I sighed, shaking my head. "It's a long story."

"And one I demand to know."

The mortification of rejection overpowered me.

Shit. Don't cry, Hannah. Don't cry!

My lips trembled, tears burning the backs of my eyes as words began to pour from my mouth. "All I want is a family. Is that so much to ask?"

"Oh, H." Karen wrapped her arms around herself. My arms immediately did the same, giving myself a hard, tight hug.

I closed my eyes, gaining comfort from the tight squeeze.

"There'd been a mix-up," I explained, careful not to mention names. "He thought it was a barbecue all you could eat. But he was a good sport and stayed the entire time. We saw each other naked. It was part of the therapy."

"Oh. Was he built?" Chrissy asked, her voice slightly breathless.

"No. He had a belly." I blinked my eyes open, utterly devastated as Malik's words echoed in my ears. "He said he's what they call strong-fat."

"And that distresses you?"

"No. It's that I wanted to kiss his belly. I never want to kiss *anything*."

"I think you mean anyone," Karen said with a small grin. "But let's return to the desire. You didn't like the feeling?"

"No, I did. I wanted to do it."

And that's the problem.

Karen cringed. "Mistress... did you offer to kiss his belly?"

I nodded glumly. "I said I was attracted to him. And that he was the first real man I'd ever been attracted to. I asked if I could kiss his belly and maybe other areas."

They both winced.

"And he said...?"

"That he was good." His rejection still stung, cutting me deep. "Then he turned and went into his meat hut, and that was the last I saw of him."

"Alright, we need to talk more about the meat huts but... Mistress, you get why he acted that way, right?" Karen asked softly.

I glumly nodded. "I've analysed the situation and understand that I can't proposition people based on where I would like to kiss them."

She nodded. "Good. What will you do differently the next time this happens?"

I paused, hesitating. "Perhaps offer to take him to dinner first?"

"Great! That's a great option."

"I should apologise. Do you think sending cookies would be well accepted?"

"Cookies are always a good option," Chrissy said with a wise nod.

"Okay. Cookies it is."

A little bell rang in my ear—our sign that it was time to wrap up the show.

"And on that note, that's it for our show today," Karen said, closing down the podcast. "If you'd like to know more about any of the adventures we did, check out our social media and website. In the meantime, have a nasty day."

She hit our theme song, and I stared at my

hands as it played, ending our recording for this week. We chatted about Karen's upcoming date then it was her turn to grill me.

"Now," Karen said, leaning in toward the camera. "When are you going to take him those cookies? And can I know his name?"

I shook my head slowly. "Maybe tomorrow. And no, not yet."

"Absolutely tomorrow," Chrissy directed with a slap of her hand. "You're fixating on this. Fix it, and you can move on."

I blew out a breath. "You're right. I'll fix it."

Cookies, an apology, and a promise to never proposition him again.

Hopefully, that would fix what I might have broken.

"Good." With a nod, Chrissy sat back. "Now, my turn for help. Do we like Veraminta or Philodrena better for names?" She asked, patting her pregnant belly. "Cause I like—"

"Hell to the no is my goddaughter being called either of them. They are good names for other people. I thought we agreed on—"

I listened with one ear as Karen and Chrissy began to fight over names, my thoughts a couple of miles away, thinking of one very attractive police officer who loved cookies.

Apology, cookies, and a promise. I can do this.

5

Malik

"Hey, have you guys heard from Hannah?"

I looked up from my paperwork, eyebrows raising. "Sharp?"

"Yeah." Jane, one of the station's dispatchers, nodded. "She normally does her cookie delivery on Mondays, Wednesdays, and Fridays. Only, she hasn't been this week. Occasionally she might miss a day—but a whole week?" She shook her head. "Unusual."

"Shit." Paulette, one of our best detectives, pushed to a stand. "You're right. I didn't see her at the park this week either. We should go do a welfare check."

The Sheriff poked his head out of his office. "Did I hear 'welfare check'? Who's the citizen?"

"Hannah Sharp," Jane said before I could stop her. "She hasn't delivered any cookies this week."

"Shit, I thought she was on holiday. Didn't she say anything at the last drop-off?"

"Nothing about a holiday. And she said I'd see her Monday when she dropped off last Friday's batch," Jane supplied helpfully.

"Normally calls if she's sick too," Caleb added, rubbing his chin. "Malik, you know anything?"

My tongue felt too big for my mouth as I glanced around the bullpen.

Only that I embarrassed her and despite my best efforts she never seems to be home when I stop in?

"I'll drive out now if you don't mind, Sheriff? My shift's nearly up anyway," I offered.

Tristan waved his hand in my direction. "Go. Call us once you know."

"Will do." I reached for my jacket, catching Caleb's eye as I shrugged it on. "What?"

"Nothing." A knowing grin lit his face. "Tell Hannah hi from me."

I rolled my eyes, flicking him the bird. "It's a welfare check, you dick."

"Hey." He held up his hands. "No judgment."

I waggled a finger in his direction. "And not a word to my sister."

His grin widened. "My fiancé is not someone I keep secrets from."

"Not a secret if you just forget to tell her."

The rat-bastard traitor had the gall to laugh. "Yeah, that's not gonna happen."

I caught my keys, tucking them into my back pocket. "You know, marrying my sister was meant to be a good thing. I can revoke my blessing at any time."

"But you wouldn't because you love me."

I twisted, calling over my shoulder as I exited the bullpen. "You wish!"

Hannah lived in a coastal bungalow just north of town. Buried in suburbia, it was a little blink and you'd miss it place, surrounded by old trees and creeper vines. I'd only ever been inside Hannah's house once, a few years ago when I'd returned a stack of plates and linen kitchen towels that she always used to wrap the cookies in. When I'd asked her why she'd explained that she didn't like using plastics because they weren't biodegradable.

I parked the cruiser on her curb, pausing for a moment to gaze at the house. Orderly but overlooked. It seemed to be a metaphor for the woman who lived inside. I'd heard her called mean for years, but I'd never thought of her as such. Hannah didn't know how to be anything but direct—and I appreciated that aspect of her personality. Even in this small town, we dealt with our fair share of dirtbags (mostly tourists) who seemed to be trying to make lying an art form.

At her door, I lifted a hand, knocking out a quick rhythm on her door. The smell of cookies hung heavy in the air.

Oh, she's definitely home.

Silence greeted my knock.

"Hannah?" I called, knocking again. "Hannah, it's Malik. You alright in there? The station is worried about you. You haven't been by all week. Hannah?"

I couldn't hear anything inside. Not music, not movement, nothing except the smell of cookies.

"If you don't answer, I'm coming in."

Still no movement.

"Fine," I muttered. "If that's how you want to play it."

I began to search around her porch, looking for a hidden spare key.

"Ah-ha!" I pulled the fake succulent out of its pot, finding the key in the bottom. "I'm adding a talk about security to our agenda."

"Agenda?"

I spun, key in one hand, succulent held aloft in the other, finding Hannah standing on the bottom step of her porch.

"You're okay?"

Hannah tipped her head to one side, her long curtain of hair falling in a perfect cascade. "Was that in question?"

"Cookies!" I burst out, words once again failing me as the image of her naked body with her pink little nipples and the soft dark hair at her—

"Cookies?" Hannah asked, flicking her hair back. "What about cookies?"

"You haven't been by the station in a week. We were worried."

"Because you didn't have any cookies?"

I shook my head, more than aware of the fact I was fucking this up. "Shit. Here, let me help you with that."

I tossed the key and succulent back in the pot and reached for the loaded tote bags in her hands.

"Oh, thank you."

I heaved them up, tailing her as she unlocked her door and entered the house.

White walls, warm wood floors, and soft furnishings graced the space—her room both comfortable and inviting.

"Nice place, new painting?" I asked, nodding at the giant image over her fireplace—under which proudly sat the junk Halloween trophy.

"No. It's an original Jefferson. It's fifty—oh." Hannah paused, sending me' big eyes. "You meant, is it a new purchase."

"Yeah. But tell me more. Jefferson? Never heard of him."

"Her," she corrected. "Ms. Anna Jefferson was a revolutionary water artist. When this came up for sale, I knew I had to have it."

I nodded, impressed by the gentle brush strokes and use of colour that implied depth to the mother and her cradled baby.

"Nice purchase."

"Thank you. You can put the bags in the kitchen."

I followed her to the kitchen and froze. Cookies lined every available surface, while stacks of linen-covered plates were piled on her dinner table.

"Um... where would you like these?"

"Just on the floor, thank you."

I dropped the bags then bent, automatically beginning to unpack the contents.

Flour, milk, butter, eggs, chocolate, chocolate, chocolate....

"Hannah?"

"Yeah?"

"Are you making *more* cookies?"

She hesitated, one hand buried in the other tote. "Yes?"

I raised an eyebrow. "Is that a question?"

She shook her head, a worrying little frown marring her brow. "Yes, I'm making more cookies."

I gestured at the cookie heaven around us. "Do you need more cookies?"

She worried her bottom lip, nodding.

"Hannah... what's going on?"

For a moment, she crouched beside me, her body frozen, her face a picture of conflicted confusion.

"I...." She hesitated, appearing uncertain.

"Hey." I reached out to squeeze her hand, then froze, my fingers hovering a fraction above hers. "Shit, no touching. Sorry."

That seemed to snap her into movement. She scooped the cold items up, juggling the products as she tugged the fridge open, shoving them onto the various shelves.

"Hannah, what the fuck?"

I rose as she shoved the door closed, pressing her back against it, her eyes wide as she stared up at me.

"Malik?"

I hesitated, unsure of the tone in her voice. "Yeah, babe?"

"The cookies are for you. I need to apologise, but I also want you to kiss me."
My head spun.
"What?"
"Kiss me."

6

Hannah

Malik stared at me for a beat.

"I'm sorry," he repeated. "What?"

I could hear my heart beating in my chest. My stomach twisted, my palms suddenly clammy.

"I know you don't like me but could you please kiss me?"

"Don't—what?" he repeated for the third time.

I swallowed, attempting to draw moisture into my mouth. "I've never been kissed. I'm not sure if I'll like it. But I can't stop thinking of you touching me. Of Halloween and your hands and your belly and—"

"Stop." He held up both hands. "Okay, I think we have a fundamental misunderstanding here."

My heart dropped, tears burning at the back of my eyes.

"Hannah, you said you don't like to be touched."

I nodded. "I don't. Normally."

Malik crossed his arms over his impressive chest, one eyebrow cocked in question. "What do you mean by 'normally'?"

I hesitated, unsure of how much I could trust him. How much I wanted to reveal.

"I don't like to be touched. Kids are okay, they don't have secondary motives. But adults? There's always something they want from you."

He hesitated. "Did someone hurt you?"

I paused, trying to work out how to translate what I felt into words he could understand.

"Not in the way you are thinking. My parents... well, they used physical touch as a weapon. Hugs, kisses, brushing my hair. They performed these tasks in front of each other or others, not because they wanted to but because it made them seem like good people. As a result, I don't trust touch. I can't. But with you?" I sighed, closing my eyes, remembering Halloween. "With you it's different."

"How is it different?" His voice was low, gruff,

a weird tension running through it. "Explain it to me."

I shook my head slowly, unable to put into words the way he made me feel. "I don't know. It's just... different."

Malik began to walk toward me, his stride slow but purposeful. "Good different or bad different?"

"Good," I whispered, our gazes locked.

"When you asked me to stop on Halloween, was it because my touch felt bad?"

I shook my head as he drew closer, his chest only an inch from mine.

"How did it feel, Hannah? Good or bad?"

"Amazing," I admitted. "Overwhelming. I didn't want you to stop but I couldn't control the —the—the—feelings you caused."

"Feelings? What kind of feelings, Hannah-mine?"

My heart stuttered in my chest at his whispered endearment.

"The good kind. The kind that made me go home and self-pleasure."

Malik shuddered, his arms shot out, hands pressing flat to the fridge door on either side of my head.

"Can I touch you, Hannah? Will you let me?"

I searched his face, searched his expression

for any kind of artifice or dishonesty—finding only desire.

"Please."

With a groan, Malik closed his eyes, his head tilting backward. "Shit. Give me a moment."

He stepped back, reaching for the radio on his shoulder rattling off a series of codes too quick for me to catch easily. Dispatch radioed back with an affirmative.

"What did you tell them?" I asked, curious as he turned the radio off.

"That everything is good and I'm off duty and they're not to bother me."

"Oh."

With that completed, his hands returned to their position on the fridge, his body leaning in until he stood less than a breath away from me.

"Now, where were we?"

I tilted my head back a little, my heart fluttering hopefully. "You were thinking of kissing me?"

"Oh, Hannah-mine, I'm not thinking of kissing you, I'm *going* to kiss you."

And with that declaration he leaned in, closing the gap between us, easing his lips over mine.

Oh. Oh, my.

Malik's lips were firm as he peppered soft

kisses along my own—the sensation unusual and utterly delightful. Liquid heat pooled low in my abdomen; a delicious lethargy began to invade my limbs.

Is this desire? Is this what I've been missing?

Malik pulled back a fraction, a teasing grin tilting his lips. "You know, you can kiss back."

"Oh!" My hands reach out, fisting his shirt. "I'm sorry. It's just—I didn't realise—that is—I haven't done this before."

Malik raised an eyebrow. "What? Kiss against your fridge?"

"All of it."

Malik froze. "All... do you mean kissing?"

I nodded.

"And... *all*?"

I nodded again.

He sucked in a breath. "But Hannah you're...."

"Weird?" I prompted when he didn't continue. "Frigid? Cold? Mean?"

"Wonderful. Gorgeous. Amazing. Perfect," he corrected. "Stop talking about yourself that way?"

My heart gave that little flutter I now associated with Malik.

"Are you comfortable with me kissing you?" Malik asked, his hand reaching out to capture a strand of my hair.

"Yes."

"How about me touching you?" he asked, his hand dropping the strand to brush against my shoulder.

"Definitely."

"Good. Is there anything you don't want me to do? Do we need a safeword?"

Excitement sparked at his words. "Safeword? You're familiar with BDSM?"

His eyebrows shot up. "I mean... I guess so. Sure."

"Oh, thank goodness." I reached over, hesitating for a moment then captured his hand with mine, slipping out from under his arm and pulling him after me.

"Follow me."

"Okay."

I guided him down the hall to my second bedroom, pausing with one hand on the door handle.

"My safeword is Gemini," I told him. "What's yours?"

"Uh... I didn't realise *I'd* need one."

I rolled my eyes. "Everyone needs a safeword, Malik."

"Uh, how about Blueberry?"

I nodded, filing that away. "And you're familiar with green, orange, red?"

He shook his head slowly. "No?"

"Green is go, orange is slow, red is stop. If you ever feel unsafe or want something to end you say Blueberry. Got it?"

He nodded, his expression unreadable.

"Great!" I pushed the door open. "Let's get started."

Malik stepped through the doorway, his voice strangled as he whispered, "Oh. My. God."

7

Malik

I stared at the walls with their carefully hung implements of torture. The multiple whips and chains, the paddles and crops.

This is a kink room!

My mind felt as if it were about to explode. Hannah had said she'd never been kissed. That she hadn't even allowed a person to so much as touch her before. And yet here sat a kink room in all its kink-ish glory.

I have no words.

Hannah reached out, fingering one of the paddles. "Do you have a pain preference?"

I gulped, suddenly uncertain. "Pain—er, none?"

She turned, lifting an eyebrow. "Wait, are you being serious right now?"

"Blueberry," I choked out as colour fled her face.

"Malik I...." She turned away from me, her hands cupping her cheeks. "Oh, dear."

"Hannah, it's fine. I mean, if you're into this I'm cool to give it a go, it's just—"

"I'm not."

Her words cut me off. "What?"

"I'm not into this." She turned back around slowly. "Or maybe I am. I don't know. It's just...."

She made a distressed sound, her hands flicking agitatedly as she bounced on the heels of her feet.

I looked around, spotting a weirdly shaped settee. "Here, let's talk." I caught her hand, tugging her over to the seat.

Once settled, I kept her hands in my lap, my thumbs gently grazing her soft skin.

"Okay, now. Let me give a quick recap here, Hannah-mine. We barely kiss and suddenly there're paddles involved." I shot her an amused smile, hoping to reassure her. "Let's slow it down and discuss our boundaries before we dive on in."

She nodded, her face still pale.

"Alright, let's start with some getting-to-know-you questions. Have you kissed anyone before? Romantically I mean."

She shook her head.

"Engaged in sexual relations?"

"Other than with myself?"

I nodded, shifting our hands slightly so she wouldn't feel my traitorous dick hardening at that visual.

"No."

"But you're into kink?"

She hesitated. "I don't know."

"Explain it to me."

She looked anywhere but at me, her gaze flicking from wall to ceiling to floor and back.

"I want a family. I always have. Babies and a partner. Kids that I can love. Even a dog or cat or ferret—whatever they want. But the physical thing wasn't for me."

She paused, tucking a strand of hair behind her ear nervously. "Have you heard of the Wicked Women Podcast?"

I nodded. "Sure. All the women in my life love it. I've listened to a few episodes; those ladies are hilarious."

Hannah blushed. "Thank you. I'm Mistress H."

Her admission hit me like a truck to the face.

"Mistress... wow. That's incredible. Do you enjoy it?"

Hannah lifted one shoulder in a half-shrug. "Podcasting is fine. It's become massive so we get paid a lot now. It's how I was able to afford the Jefferson."

I nodded, wondering what 'a lot' meant.

"Karen, my co-host, is also my best friend. And back before we started the podcast, I told her about my issue. She suggested I look into sexuality classes where they explore alternatives to intercourse. When I learned about BDSM, I thought maybe I could become a mistress and offer my future partner gratification through means other than penile-vaginal penetration."

I swallowed. "And now?"

Hannah glanced up at me, her cheeks rosy. "Now I want penetration."

Fuck.

That shouldn't have been sexy. It shouldn't have sounded that way coming out of her mouth. It shouldn't have been naughty and delicious and dirty all at the same time.

Fuck. Fuck. Fuck.

I cleared my throat, attempting to find the words I needed.

"Hannah, can we... start slow?"

She tilted her head to one side. "Slow?"

"Mm." I pressed a hand against my chest. "I'm afraid my little heart isn't too sure about all this fancy equipment. But this?" I gestured between us. "This feels right."

She considered me with her expressive eyes. "But I heard that a real man wants—"

I cut in. "Real man? Babe, this is the second time you've referred to someone as 'real'. What are you talking about?"

"It's what my mom says. Real men want women who know how to give pleasure in the bedroom."

"Okay, one—unless we're talking about fictional characters, I'm not sure there are real and unreal men. Two—I'm telling you right now, giving and taking pleasure and an openness to communicate about likes and preferences is more important than anything else."

Hannah's perfectly sculpted eyebrows arched. "Really?"

"Uh-huh." I reached out, cupping her cheek gently. "So how about we take this nice and slow? Let's start with some kissing and dinner. We can see where the night takes us after that."

Her big blue eyes considered me, her expression a heartbreaking mixture of hope and weary caution.

"On one condition."

"Hit me with it," I encouraged.

"Can you teach me how to kiss with tongues?"

My cock, already hard, stood to attention.

"Oh, Hannah-mine. We're gonna explore all that and much, much more."

8

Hannah

Malik led me from the playroom into my bedroom, nodding as he looked around.

"This is perfect."

I hesitated, my fingers itching to straighten the bedclothes or dim the lights.

"Are you sure?"

Malik turned, his hands coming to settle on my waist. "Trust me, Hannah?"

I ducked my head. "I'm trying."

"Good enough." He gently backed me up, grinning when my knees hit the back of the bed, my body automatically sitting.

"What are we doing?" I whispered into the quiet hush.

His teeth flashed as he smiled. "Learning each other."

He reached out, fingers finding my hand as he lowered himself to crouch before me. He rubbed circles along the back of my clenched fist where it lay on my thigh.

"I thought we were going to kiss." My voice sounded breathless as I became hyper-fixated on the sensation of his fingers against my skin.

"Oh, we will." He made a sound in his throat. "Patience, Hannah."

He dropped his hands down to cup my ankles, slowly moving them up my legs. Through the thin material of my leggings, I could feel the heat of his skin, the barrier somehow adding to my pleasure.

This man is dangerous.

"Can I touch you?"

He huffed out a chuckle.

"Fuck yes. Please."

I reached out, placing one hand on his shoulder, the other curling around his neck. He seemed surprised but pleased, his breath catching for a moment.

"Remember," he whispered into the hush of my bedroom. "If I do anything you don't like, your safeword is Gemini."

I nodded, unable to speak. I could feel the tension in his muscles. Could see how he held himself back as he continued to run his hands up and down my legs, getting slightly higher each time before returning back to my ankles.

I wanted to break his restraint. I wanted to force his hands away from my knees and higher to my most sensitive place, the aching bud between my legs.

I want him to play with me.

We were staring at each other, our breath mingling, gazes hot with unspoken words.

Could I?

I slowly moved my hand up until my fingers tangled in his hair.

Be bold, Hannah.

With a firm grasp, I gently pulled him toward me, our mouths meeting in a chaste kiss.

Chaste? I want heat.

I flicked my tongue against his lips, wanting so desperately to taste him as heat and want crashed into me.

Malik made a sound—a half-man-half-animal groan that seemed torn from somewhere deep within him.

His hands came up, one going to my neck, the other to my hip. With a grunt he pulled me into him, his big body settling between my legs, his mouth at the perfect height.

And oh, what a mouth. He devoured me,

our lips clashing as we clung together, tongues dancing and gliding, bodies rocking in a poor imitation of that most primal need.

He tilted my head, granting himself access to my neck. He grunted as he finished our kiss, his lips finding the sensitive spot below my ear, the erogenous zone on the seam of my neck. When he grazed his teeth against a tiny sliver of skin at my collarbone, my underwear flooded with liquid heat.

"Malik." I groaned his name, moaned it, whispered it like a prayer. Over and over, I begged for release as he feasted on me, laying waste to my body. "Malik."

Desperate to return even a fraction of the pleasure I was receiving, I thrust a hand between us, reaching down to brush fingers against his crotch. He made a noise, a harsh sound as he shifted, reaching down to press my hand hard against his erect length.

Oh, Gods.

I needed him to touch me. I wanted his hands, his mouth, his tongue on me and in me. I wanted him to feel and touch every part of me.

I want to kiss his belly.

He peeled my shirt from my body as his mouth returned to mine, our tongues dancing.

More.

"Malik." I panted.

"Fuck." He hooked his arms under my knees, lifting me easily as he rose, turned, and sat back on the bed, allowing me to slide down his solid body until my ass sat firmly in his lap. "Better?

"Definitely."

He gazed down at my breasts, his groan rumbling through me. "I can't decide which breast to worship first."

I unhooked my bra, tossing it free then pressed my breasts together. "Why not both?"

He muttered a curse, his head dropping to lick and suck, his fingers teasing over and over.

Malik. Malik. Malik.

His name became the beat of my heart as he played with my body, stripping me of clothes and apprehension.

He dropped a hand to my leggings, hesitating for a moment.

"Gonna touch you now."

"Please do."

With a chuckle he brushed aside fabric, his hand sliding along the skin of my abdomen to tangle in my soft curls.

"Hannah, where are your panties?"

I chuckled, rocking against him. "I didn't feel like wearing any today."

"You naughty little sprite." His fingers dipped, both of us gasping.

"Fuck. So wet." He grunted, shifting us slightly to gain better access. "Can't wait to taste you."

"Malik!" I gasped, as he pressed against my clit.

"Mm? Should I stop?"

"Green! Green, green, green!" I cried, my hips beginning to rock urgently against him. With a dark chuckle, he played me, coaxing pleasure from my deprived body.

This is what those movies are about. And the books. All this time this is what they meant.

He shifted his finger and it was enough to tip me over the edge. My body bucked, my head falling back as pleasure-pain exploded into utterly delicious bliss.

Oh, Malik.

"Good?" he asked, cradling me against his chest.

I nodded, feeling a little drowsy. "Really good."

"Oh, only really good?" He pulled back; his grin utterly evil. "Perhaps I didn't do it right."

"Wait—what are you—?"

He twisted, dropping me onto the bed, his hands reaching for my leggings and quickly removing them from my body.

"Guess I'll just have to work out what I'm doing wrong and then keep trying until I get it right."

"Malik I—" My mouth snapped shut, my body arching as his mouth covered me.

"Malik!"

9

Malik

I feasted, memorising Hannah's taste. Her cries. What made her shiver and quake.

"Malik! I want more."

"More?" I asked, my face covered in her arousal. "How much more?"

She pushed up on her elbows, her face flushed and pink. "All of you."

Something primal hit me in my gut. "We should wait...."

"No." She shook her head vehemently. "No more waiting. I'm thirty-one years old. I want this. Now."

Well, when you put it like that.

I stood, beginning to strip off my clothing,

careful to remove my belt and place my weapons and equipment in a safe area.

As I unbuttoned my shirt and revealed my stomach, Hannah sighed dreamily.

"Like what you see?" I asked with a grin.

"Mm, very much."

I stripped off my pants and underwear quickly, gratified to find her eyes locked on my cock.

"Can I...?" she asked, her hand held out toward me.

"Fuck yes."

With some hesitancy, she reached out, her fingers grazing along the length of me.

Fucking hell that feels good.

Her tongue poked out as she tasted me, catching a drop of precum. My hand cupped the back of her head, pressing her against me, desperate for more.

"Fuck, Hannah-mine. Yes! Feels fucking amazing."

My praise spurred her on, her lips parting as she leaned forward, taking more of my thick length in her hot little mouth.

Saints above. I've died and gone to heaven.

The angel in front of me bobbed her head, her mouth a wicked delight as she robbed me of speech.

Pressure built in my lower back, the urge to come down her throat became overwhelming.

"Fuck, Hannah. Gonna need you to stop if you want more. Baby... I can't...."

With a lip-smacking pop, she pulled away, rocking back on the bed.

"Was that okay?"

I blinked at her as if she were crazy.

"Okay? Okay? Babe, that was fucking perfect."

She flushed, a pleased little smile lighting her face. "I liked it too."

"Anytime you want to get me all hot and bothered, just remind me of that."

She grinned. "Noted."

Then she did something surprising. Or perhaps not so, if I reflected on what had led us to this moment.

Hannah leaned forward and kissed my stomach.

As predicted, her breasts cradled my cock, her hair soft as it brushed my thighs, her lips peppering sweet kisses along my waistline.

"I love this," she whispered against my skin. "I love all of you, Malik."

Once again, Hannah hit me like a ton of bricks.

Mine. Wow. This woman is mine. She is it for me.

Caleb's never gonna let me hear the end of this.

Unsurprisingly, I didn't care. I just wanted this woman. Now. Badly.

"I love you, Hannah-mine."

She startled, her body recoiling as she looked up at me, eyes wide and shocked.

"What?"

"I said I love you."

"But why?"

I blinked. "Why?"

"Yes. Is it because we're about to have sexual relations?"

I chuckled. "Babe, we are having sexual relations."

"Penetration then."

"No." I dropped back to the floor, wrapping my arms around her. "It's because you're freaking amazing, Hannah Sharp. You and your cookies, and your caring, and your secret life as a podcaster. The way you look after people without them even knowing. I find you utterly enchanting, and I want to spend the rest of my life getting to know every part of who you are."

I watched as a million emotions crossed Hannah's face.

"But we haven't even had sex yet."

I burst out laughing. "Sex or no sex, this love I feel isn't gonna change."

She seemed to process that. "Am I in love?"

"Don't know," I said cheerfully. "I hope so, one day. But it's okay. I got enough love for the both of us." I leaned in, kissing her nose. "And if this works out long-term, which it will, then I can be the one to say I've always loved you more."

Her lips twitched, tilting up at the corners. "You're teasing me about this."

"Never!" I declared, hooking my arms under her knees and lifting her further onto the bed, my body quickly covering hers.

"Malik!" She squealed, laughing as I pressed tiny kisses all over her beautiful face. "Malik!"

She cupped my face, holding me still for a moment, her gaze sweeping my face, searching for... something. Whatever it was, she must have found it because the next thing I knew, she was kissing me—our tongues tangling, our breaths mingling, our bodies sinking into each other as hands roamed and desire took over.

"Come in me," she whispered.

"Fuck. Condom?"

She wiggled out from under me, her breasts bouncing enticingly as she leaned over, pulling an unopened box from the bedside table.

I couldn't help but lean in, capturing one of her perky pink nipples in my mouth as I took over, ripping the box open and pulling a bunch free.

I rocked back, sadly forced to let go of Hannah's delicious breast as I concentrated on ripping the packet and rolling the condom on.

"Now?" Hannah asked, shifting to spread her thighs wide, granting me an uninterrupted view of her pretty pussy.

"Oh no," I whispered. "Let me get you ready first."

I crawled up the bed to drop my head back at her pussy, whispering sweet praises as my lips and tongue played across her seam.

"Malik," she moaned, arching against me as my tongue dipped, sweeping across her clit—finding all her secrets.

"Let me hear you," I murmured, pulling back slightly to press a kiss to her inner thigh. "I want to hear how much you're enjoying this, Hannah."

She let out another breathless moan as my mouth returned, all my focus on her pleasure. I circled and pressed, sucked and licked, finding a pace and rhythm that had her creaming under me again and again, her thighs clenching my head every time she came, her taste soaking my face.

A man could die happy here.

"Please," she finally begged, her body now in constant movement under my mouth. "I need more, Malik!"

I chuckled.

"So greedy, Hannah-mine."

With one finger pressing against her entrance, I flicked my tongue against her clit as I slipped it inside, stretching her.

"Malik!"

Hannah shattered under me, her orgasm sending her arching off the bed, a wet rush coating my face as she fell apart, gasping and scratching—a wildcat.

I rested my chin on her abdomen, inordinately pleased to have been the man to give her this first time.

"That was...." She searched for the words.

"Brilliant, spectacular, world-shattering?" I offered.

"Adequate but not what I wanted."

I blinked. "Excuse me?"

"I want you in me, Malik. That was very good for oral, I'm sure. But I'm empty and aching. I want you in me. I want you to fuck me."

I sat frozen for a moment, doubts assailing me. Then I saw her lips begin to curl up at the corners.

"Oh, you evil woman!"

I surged up the bed, tickling her relentlessly.

"Adequate? Adequate, Hannah? I'll show you adequate."

I pinned her down, my cock pressing against her entrance, both of us stilling.

"Ready, babe?"

She nodded, reaching down to grasp my cock in her hand.

My eyes nearly crossed as she pulled me closer.

"Now."

I pushed forward, working my thick length into her tight snatch, feeling the barrier give way as I thrust inside.

Fuck. Fuck she's tiny. Fuck.

She gasped, and I paused, giving her time to adjust.

"Shit, Hannah. Fuck you're amazing. Feel okay? Shit, speak to me, Hannah."

Her head had fallen back, her lids closed as she bit her lip.

"It feels...."

I braced.

"More than adequate."

I huffed out a laugh, dropping my head to nip at her lips. "More being good?"

"Oh, yes. Very, very good."

"But not mind-blowing?"

She peeked up at me. "Not yet, but I have hope."

"You cheeky brat."

I moved, just a little, testing to see how she'd react.

Her hands gripped my sides, urging me on.

I began to press kisses to her cheeks, her lips, sucking gently at her neck as I began to move, thrusting slowly into her, moving with purpose.

Pleasure. I want Hannah's pleasure.

"Feel so fucking good." I heaped praise on my woman as her pussy clutched my cock. "Tight. Hot. So, fucking good. So fucking good."

"Malik."

I heard the plea in her voice, the need.

I quickened my pace, shifting to allow me to work a hand between us.

"What are you—" Hannah bit off her question as my fingers found her clit.

"Ohmigods! Malik, Malik, Malik, Malik!"

Hannah shattered, her hot pussy milking my cock. I tried desperately to hang on, to prevent the rollercoaster of need from overwhelming me, but it was her whispered admission that sent me over the edge.

"I love you."

With brutal thrusts, I came, fucking her with an intensity I'd never felt before. She took it, thrilling in my animalistic need, her lips sinking into the seam of my shoulder, marking me as I collapsed onto her.

We stayed like that for a long moment, sweaty and deliciously wrecked.

"Stay for dinner?" she asked softly, hesitantly.

"Babe, you couldn't get rid of me if you tried."

Hannah cupped my cheek. "Do you mean that?"

I nodded.

"Then maybe... if you'd like... do you want to stay forever?"

My eyebrows lifted, and something clicked deep in my soul.

"Hannah Sharp, are you proposing to me?"

She bit her lip. "Maybe?"

"In that case—yes! Fuck yeah, I'll marry you."

I rolled us, pulling her on top of me. "Never gonna be rid of me now."

"Good."

EPILOGUE 1

Malik

"This is...." Jane looked around at the cookie stockpile that currently dominated the precinct's break room.

"Too much?" Hannah asked, worrying her bottom lip.

"Fucking awesome!" She reached out to wrap an arm around her but I easily intercepted, pulling her into my side before Jane could touch her.

"My woman is awesome," I said with pride, pressing a kiss to her forehead. "Now. Are we ready?"

Hannah nodded.

With a grin, I led her out into the visitor

parking lot where our family and friends had assembled.

Hannah and I had watched *Brooklyn 99* a few months ago—I was slowly introducing her to the joys of comedic cop shows—and she'd fallen in love with Jake and Amy's wedding.

So, in a desperate bid to please my fiancé, I'd planned this wedding.

We walked together down the aisle to where the Sheriff stood with our bridal party. My best men—Caleb, Wolf, and my sister, on my side. Karen, Chrissy, and Chrissy's little daughter on Hannah's.

The parking lot had been transformed into a wonderland of fairy lights, fabric, and flowers.

Hand-in-hand we arrived at the end of the aisle, Tristan welcoming us to the ceremony.

"I've been instructed to welcome both the dearly beloved and the not-so-beloved here to-day," Tristan said with a laugh. "So welcome to the wedding of Malik and Hannah."

I felt disconnected from this moment, focusing so intently on Hannah's joy that I lost all sense of time and place. I said things, repeated vows, promising to love and obey a woman I'd already committed my soul to.

"I now pronounce you husband and wife. Hannah, you can kiss your man!"

With a laugh, my beautiful bride threw herself at me. I caught her, lifting her up and laughing as she pressed hot, delighted kisses to my mouth.

"Love you, Hannah-mine."

"Love you too. Thanks for choosing me."

"Every time."

And so began the next chapter of our fucking amazing love story.

EPILOGUE 2

Hannah

I held Agnes in my arms, whispering sweet nothings to our little girl.

"I love you," I whispered for the millionth time. "You are such a precious little gift. Thank you for choosing us as your parents."

Malik's arm dropped around my shoulder, his body perching on the bed beside me.

"Of course, she'd choose us," he told me with a scoff. "We're freaking awesome."

"Language!" I reprimanded. "She's less than four hours old. She doesn't need to be exposed to that kind of talk."

Malik chuckled, pulling me closer into his side. "She better get used to it. Have you heard the language her cousin is using? Where does a three-year-old even learn to say the F-word?"

"Caleb insists his son is trying to say fire-truck."

Malik laughed. "I know a curse when I hear one."

Agnes yawned, her little mouth making a small mew sound as she protested our noise.

"Sorry, sweetheart." Malik reached out, cupping the back of her head with his giant hand. "We'll keep it down."

We watched as she settled back in, her tiny eyelids never once blinking open.

"She's beautiful, isn't she?"

"Just like her momma."

I glanced up, finding Malik's gaze trained on me.

"I love you."

"Love you more."

"Impossible," he said, leaning down to press a kiss to my lips. "But we can decide on the winner later. Right now, let's watch our little girl sleep."

And we did just that.

My dearest greedy readers, thank you so much for reading Malik and Hannah's story. This story came

as a result of a spelling mistake, and because Hannah had a very loyal and dedicated following in my greedy reader FB group!

You can grab a bonus slice of life or continue the entire series by checking them out on my website at www.EvieMitchell.com

*If you enter the code **EBOOK10** you can get 10% off your purchase from my website.*

Be sure to also sign up for my newsletter or check out my website for more book news.

ABOUT THE AUTHOR

Evie Mitchell is a thirty-something romance author (she/her/hers) living with disability. She believes in inclusion, accessibility, and fierce romance. Her loves include steamy romance novels, her husband, their THREE sausage dogs (heaven help her), and her ever-growing collection of book-related mugs.

As a woman with a diverse work history including in areas such as emergency response, event management, human rights, disability access, and security - her books are filled with true stories (bridezillas), worst-case scenarios (malfunctioning dresses), and her favourite tropes (one-bed).

Evie specialises in fiercely inclusive happily ever afters.

ALSO BY EVIE MITCHELL

Capricorn Cove Series

The Shake-Up

Double the D

Muffin Top

The Mrs. Clause

New Year Knew You

Double Breasted

As You Wish

You Sleigh Me

Resolution Revolution

Meat Load

Larsson Siblings Series

Thunder Thighs

Clean Sweep

The X-list

Reality Check

The Christmas Contract

Dogg Pack Books

Puppy Love

<u>Bad English</u>

<u>The Frock Up</u>

<u>Pier Pressure</u>

All Access Series

Knot My Type

Love Flushed

Nameless Souls MC Series

<u>Runner</u>

<u>Wrath</u>

<u>Ghost</u>

<u>Shield</u>

Elliot Security Series

<u>Rough Edge</u>

<u>Bleeding Edge</u>